WELCOME TO
PASSPORT TO READING
A beginning reader's ticket to a brand-new world!

Every book in this program is designed to build read-along and read-alone skills, level by level, through engaging and enriching stories. As the reader turns each page, he or she will become more confident with new vocabulary, sight words, and comprehension.

These PASSPORT TO READING levels will help you choose the perfect book for every reader.

READING TOGETHER
Read short words in simple sentence structures together to begin a reader's journey.

READING OUT LOUD
Encourage developing readers to sound out words in more complex stories with simple vocabulary.

READING INDEPENDENTLY
Newly independent readers gain confidence reading more complex sentences with higher word counts.

READY TO READ MORE
Readers prepare for chapter books with fewer illustrations and longer paragraphs.

This book features sight words from the educator-supported Dolch Sight Words List. This encourages the reader to recognize commonly used vocabulary words, increasing reading speed and fluency.

For more information, please visit passporttoreadingbooks.com.

Enjoy the journey!

D0012342

Little, Brown and Company

Hachette Book Group
1290 Avenue of the Americas, New York, NY 10104
Visit us at lb-kids.com

Little, Brown and Company is a division of Hachette Book Group, Inc.
The Little, Brown name and logo are trademarks of Hachette Book Group, Inc.

The publisher is not responsible for websites (or their content)
that are not owned by the publisher.

First Edition: June 2015

Library of Congress Control Number: 2015905035

ISBN 978-0-316-25671-1

10 9 8 7 6 5 4 3 2 1

CW

PRINTED IN THE UNITED STATES OF AMERICA

Passport to Reading titles are leveled by independent reviewers applying the standards developed by Irene Fountas and Gay Su Pinnell in *Matching Books to Readers: Using Leveled Books in Guided Reading*, Heinemann, 1999.

MARVEL
ANT-MAN

I AM ANT-MAN

By Tomas Palacios

Inspired by Marvel's *Ant-Man*

Based on the Screenplay by Adam McKay & Paul Rudd

Story by Edgar Wright & Joe Cornish

Produced by Kevin Feige

Directed by Peyton Reed

L B

LITTLE, BROWN AND COMPANY
New York   Boston

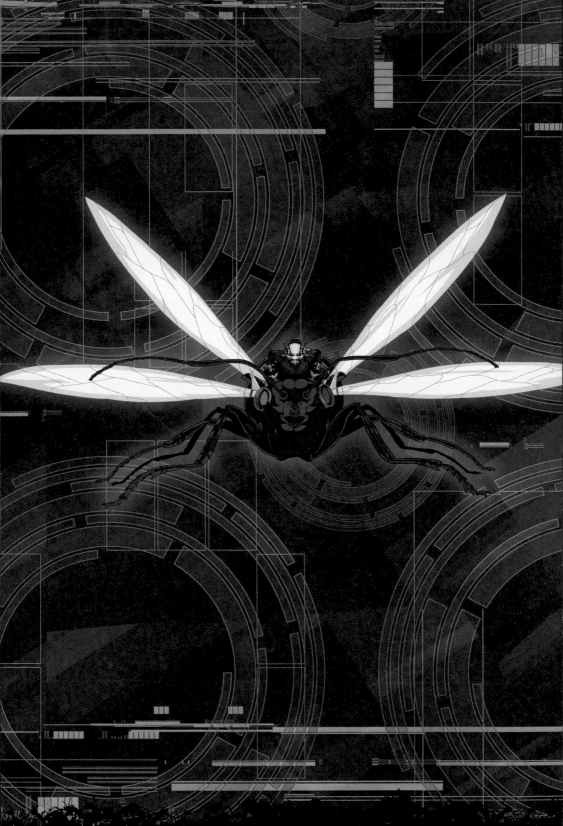

Attention, Ant-Man fans!
Look for these words
when you read this book.
Can you spot them all?

suit

helmet

bathtub

match

Scott Lang did a bad thing.
He stole a lot of money.
Scott went away for a few years,
and now he wants to be good.

Scott has a daughter.
Her name is Cassie.
He does not get to see Cassie
as much as he wants.

One day, Scott discovers a secret room.

What is inside?

It is a black-and-red suit
and a shiny helmet!
But what are they for?

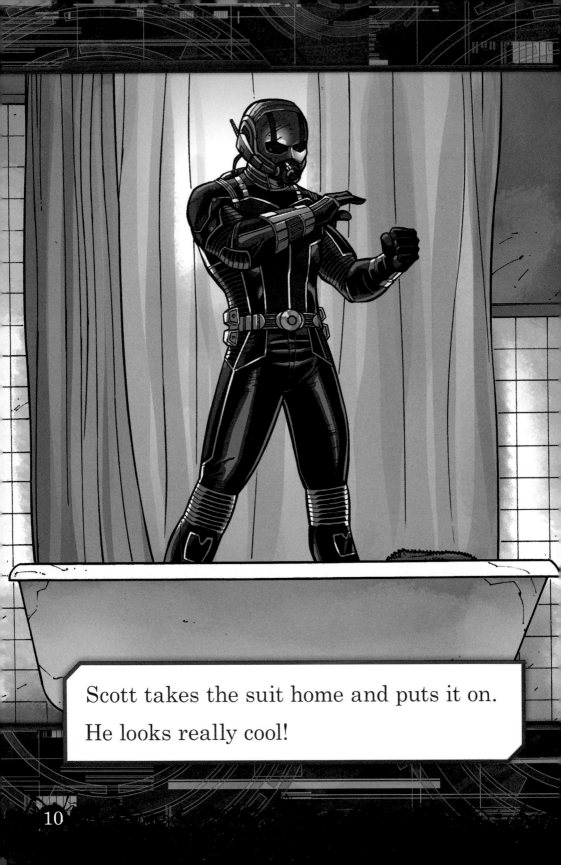

Scott takes the suit home and puts it on.
He looks really cool!

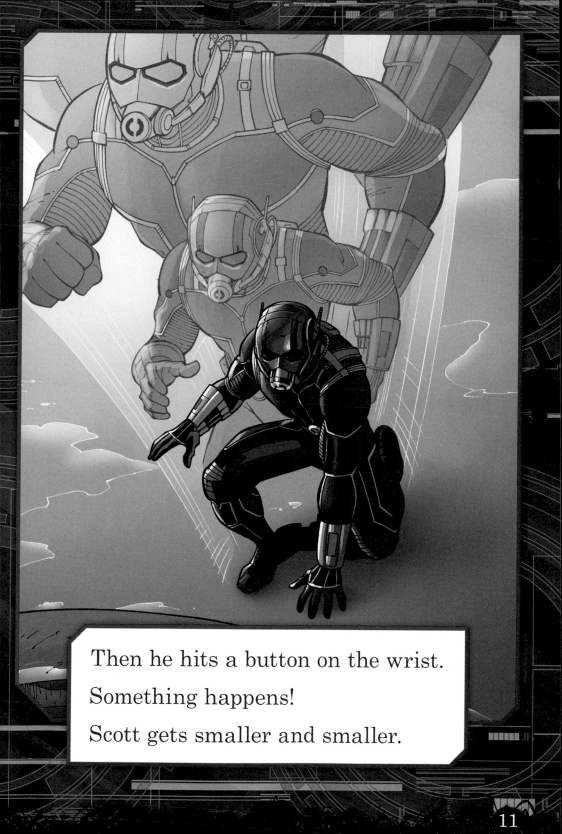

Then he hits a button on the wrist.
Something happens!
Scott gets smaller and smaller.

Scott is the size of an ant and is inside the bathtub! He sees a new world, and everything around him is bigger than before.

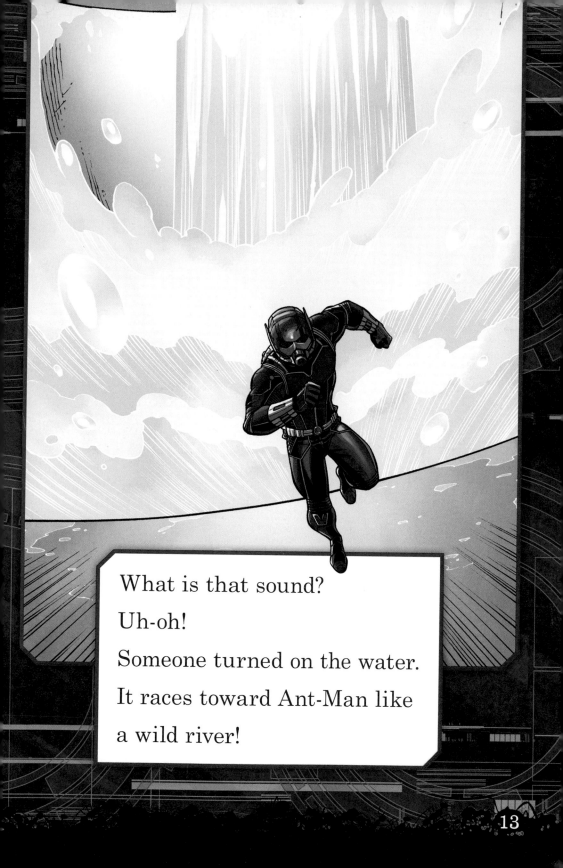

What is that sound?

Uh-oh!

Someone turned on the water.

It races toward Ant-Man like

a wild river!

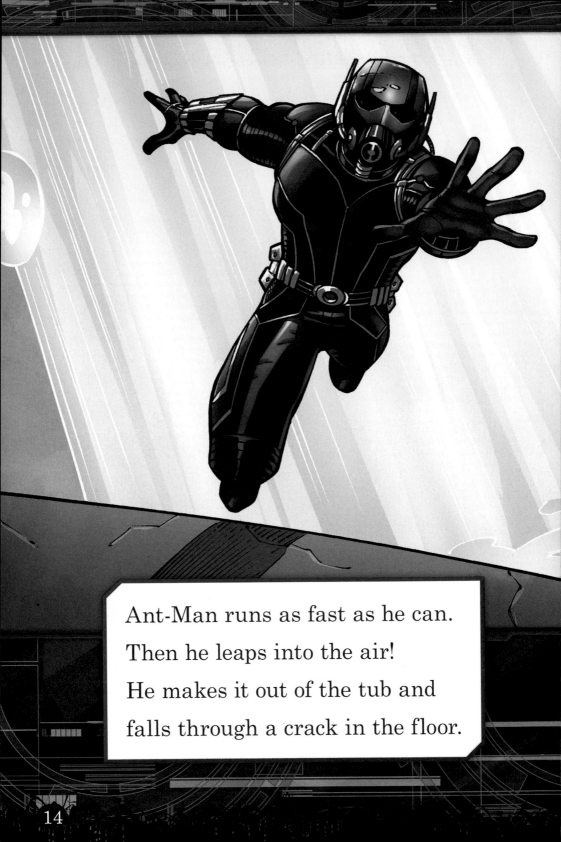

Ant-Man runs as fast as he can.
Then he leaps into the air!
He makes it out of the tub and
falls through a crack in the floor.

Ant-Man lands in the apartment below.
He tries to be very quiet
so he does not bother the puppy.
But the puppy hears Ant-Man.
He gets up to chase him!

Ant-Man learns he is faster when he is small.
He escapes the puppy and lands on something that spins and spins and spins! What is it?

It is a record player!
Ant-Man is in the
middle of a party!
People dance all around him.
Ant-Man needs to be careful.
One stomp and he will be
flattened like a bug!

Ant-Man escapes the giant feet and runs to the next apartment. He is now face-to-face with a vacuum cleaner!

Ant-Man gets sucked into the machine!
He spins and twists and ends up
in the dust bag.
It is full of crumbs and dirt the size
of gigantic rocks!
How will he get out?

The woman vacuuming shakes the bag up and down. Ant-Man shoots out the side! He rockets across the room!

Ant-Man lands on a car with a hard thump! He dents the roof! Ant-Man learns he is tougher when he is small!

Ant-Man soon sees
a group of ants.
They circle around him.

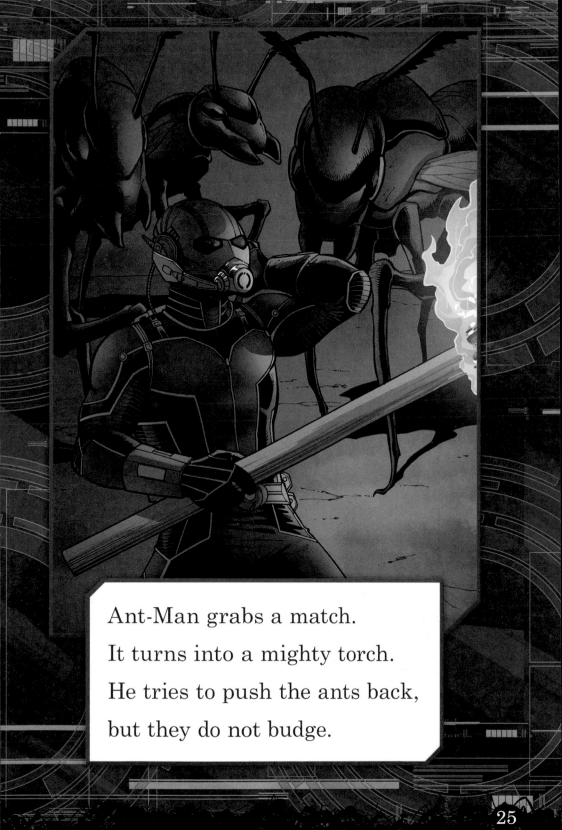

Ant-Man grabs a match.
It turns into a mighty torch.
He tries to push the ants back,
but they do not budge.

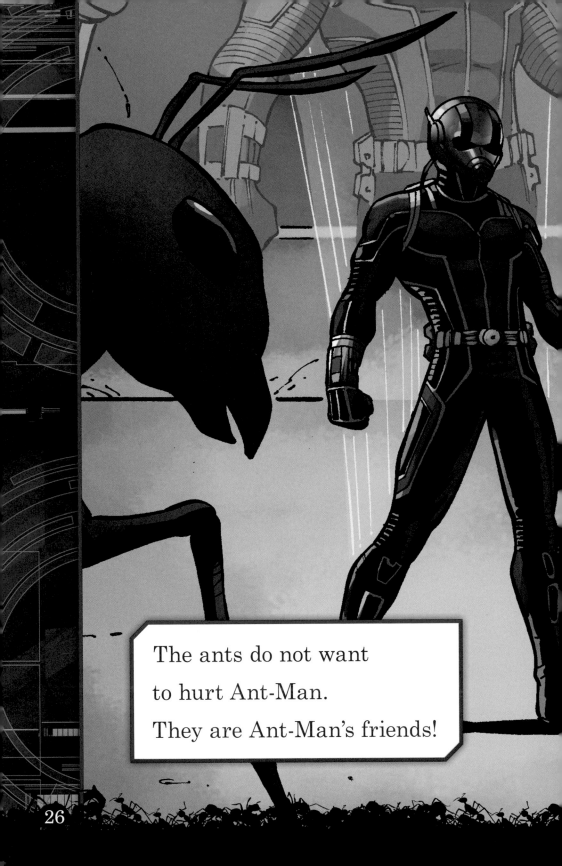

The ants do not want
to hurt Ant-Man.
They are Ant-Man's friends!

Ant-Man learns he has the power to talk to insects! They will do what he says!

Now Ant-Man has an army of ants!
Ant-Man climbs onto one.
His name is Ant-Thony.
He leads the charge!
The ants fly away!

Ant-Man protects Cassie from a bully.
Ant-Man does not like bullies.

Ant-Man does like fun!

What Ant-Man likes most
is protecting Cassie.
Ant-Man feels good.
He is a real Super Hero!